Mater and the Ghost Light

PaRragon

Bath · New York · Singapore · Hong Kong · Cologne · Delhi
Melbourne · Amsterdam · Johannesburg · Auckland · Shenzhen

This edition published by Parragon in 2011

Parragon
Queen Street House
4 Queen Street
Bath BA1 1HE, UK

Adapted by Andrea Posner-Sanchez
Illustrated by Bud Luckey and Dominique Louis

ISBN 978-1-4454-2407-1
Printed in China

Mater and the Ghost Light

Adapted by
Andrea Posner-Sanchez

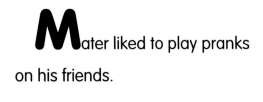

Mater liked to play pranks on his friends.

HARAAAH!

Scary pranks were his favourites!

HEEYAA!

'Oh, buddy,' Mater said to McQueen with a chuckle. 'You looked like you just seen the Ghost Light!'

'What's that?' McQueen asked.

Sheriff came forward and told the story of the mysterious blue light that haunted Radiator Springs. 'It all started on a night like tonight. A young couple were headed down this very stretch of the Mother Road when they spotted an unnatural blue glow ... and before long, all that was left were two out-of-state licence plates!'

'Don't be too scared, buddy. It ain't real,' Mater whispered to McQueen.

'It *is* real!' shouted Sheriff. 'And the one thing
that angers the Ghost Light more than anything
else ... is the sound of clanking metal!'

11

When Sheriff finished his story, the townsfolk said goodnight and quickly drove home.

Mater was left all alone—in the dark.

Gulp!

The scared tow truck drove to his shack in the junkyard. Mater thought he saw a monster in the shadows, but it was just a gnarled tree. He was trembling and shaking so much that his one good headlight fell off and broke.

Mater gasped as he saw a small glowing light
heading towards him.

'OH, NO!

It's the Ghost Light!'

The light flew right up to Mater's face. He opened one eye to peek at it.

'Oh, it's just a lightnin' bug,' he said with a nervous laugh. 'And anyhow, Sheriff said the Ghost Light is blue.'

'The Ghost Light's right behind me!' Mater screamed.

'Now it's in front of me!' he gasped.

Mater raced through the tractor field.

24

He sped past Willys Butte.

But he couldn't get away from the Ghost Light.

A very tired Mater finally came to a stop and saw that the Ghost Light was just a lantern hanging from his tow cable. 'Hey, wait a minute ...'

'**Gotcha!**' McQueen said with a smile.

'Shoot,' said Mater. 'I knowed this was a joke

the whole time.'

'You see, son, the only thing to be scared of out here is your imagination,' Sheriff told him.

'Yup. That and, of course, the *Screamin' Banshee.'* added Doc.

'THe SCReamin' WHat?!?'